The picture below
shows a Chinese set of
the nineteenth century

The knight piece
above is from a
special Staunton set
of the mid-nineteenth
century made by
Jacques.

*Chess always looks a very difficult game. Each different piece moves in its own way, and every move is planned a long way ahead. But just because it is such a logical game, it isn't nearly so hard to learn as you would think. This book will teach you chess step by step, each one illustrated both by diagram and photograph so that you can see exactly what is happening. And by the end of the book, you will be playing chess!*

*Acknowledgments*

The chess board and chess pieces shown in play, and the chess clock shown in this book, appear by courtesy of the Chess Centre, London. The computerised chess board—Chess Challenger 7—shown on page 51 appears by courtesy of Spectrum Marketing Ltd, London, and the video chess game on page 51 by courtesy of Waddington's Videomaster Ltd. The nineteenth century pieces on the front endpaper are shown by courtesy of Messrs C Barrett and Co., Burlington Arcade, London. The illustration on page 49 is by A S Leonard, and the chess problem on page 53 is by Ian Thewlis. Cover photograph by Tim Clark.

# Chess

by JEAN PICKLES
photographs by JOHN MOYES

Ladybird Books Loughborough

# Introduction

Chess is not new. It has fascinated people for hundreds of years and some very great people have been chess players, including the emperor Napoleon.

Where and when did it start? No one knows for certain, but it is now widely believed that it was invented in India about the sixth century AD, and spread from there to Western Europe. It probably reached Britain in the eleventh century. Some changes were made to the rules in the fifteenth century, giving us the game in its present form. In all its long history it has never been so popular as it is today.

The game itself is a medieval battle between two royal households, each trying to trap the other's king. It is played by two players only, on a board with sixty-four squares: a draughts board will do. It should be placed so that each player has a white square in the bottom right-hand corner of the board. One player has the white pieces and the other has the black ones. The players move alternately and the player with the white pieces always has the first move. No one is allowed to miss a move at chess.

Another important rule of chess to mention is the touch move rule. Once a player has touched a piece he must move it, and if he has put it down and taken his hand off it, then the move is complete and he cannot change his mind.

Each player has sixteen chessmen: eight pieces and eight pawns. These do not all move the same way. There

**BISHOPS** **KINGS** **QUEENS**

**NIGHTS** **ROOKS** **PAWNS**

are five different sorts of pieces, each with its own particular way of moving, and the pawns too have their own way of moving. These moves are very quickly learnt.

# Setting up the board

The rows of squares going across a chess board are called *ranks*, and the rows of squares going up and down are called *files*. To begin the game, each player sets up his pieces on the back rank as shown in the picture, with his pawns in front of them. Don't forget, there must always be a white square in the right-hand bottom corner.

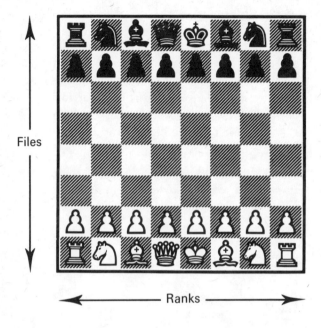

Files

Ranks

The pieces in the corner of the board are the rooks, sometimes referred to as castles. Next to them, moving in along the rank, are the knights and then the bishops. In the centre, between the bishops, are the king and the queen. The queen is always placed on her own colour with the king on the square next to her. So at the start of the game, the white queen will be on a white square and the black queen on a black one.

The pawns which are on the second rank are all the same. There are eight of them, and they may be thought of as foot soldiers.

# How the pieces move
## *The Rooks*

Rooks move in straight lines either horizontally or vertically. They may go either up or down a file or across a rank but they are not allowed to do both in one move. They must make two moves in order to turn a corner. (This applies to all pieces except the knights. A knight turns a corner in making one move.)

A rook may go as many squares as the player wishes it to along a rank or a file, provided there is nothing in its way. It is not allowed to jump over other pieces. (The only piece which *is* allowed to jump is the knight.)

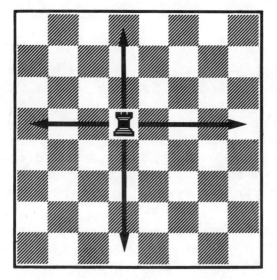

Like all the other pieces, a rook may capture an opposing piece by landing on the square occupied by the piece it is taking, not by jumping over it.

How the pieces move

# The Bishops

The bishops move diagonally in straight lines. They can move backwards or forwards and, like the rooks, they may go as many squares as the player wishes, provided there is nothing in the way. Again, they cannot jump. They capture in just the same way as rooks.

Each player starts with one bishop on a white square and another on a black square. Because they move diagonally they never leave the colour of square they start from. The bishop that starts on a white square is therefore *always* found on a white square, wherever he moves; the same applies to the bishop who starts on a black square.

How the pieces move
# The Queen

The queen can move in any direction in a straight line – horizontally or vertically as a rook moves, or diagonally as a bishop moves. From a good square she can reach so many other squares that she is by far the most powerful and valuable piece on the board.

The queen, however, has not always been so powerful. Once she could only go one square in any direction, and it was not until the rules were changed in the fifteenth century that she was given the freedom she now has.

How the pieces move
# The King

The king's moves are very limited, in the way the queen's used to be. He can move only one square in any direction. Although he does not seem a very powerful piece he is really very important indeed, because he must remain on the board. He is the only piece which cannot be captured by an opposing piece except at the end of the game. When a piece threatens to capture the king, the king is said to be *in check*, and the player must stop the check with his next move. If he cannot do this, the position is *checkmate*, and his opponent has won. The object of the game is to checkmate the opposing king.

Chess players usually say "check" when they make a move that threatens to capture their opponent's king.

The Queen's move

The Queen

The King

13

How the pieces move
# The Knight

The knight moves three squares in the shape of an L, either one square up or down and two across, or two squares up or down and one across, and it is the only piece which can jump over other pieces.

Unless it is near the edge of the board, there will always be eight squares surrounding a knight to which it can jump. It may go to any one of these squares as long as it is not occupied by a piece of the same colour. If a square *is* occupied by an opposing piece, the knight may go there by capturing the piece.

Since a knight is limited to moving only three squares at a time, it may, in some circumstances, prove much less useful than, say a rook or a bishop, which have greater freedom.

Because of their L-shaped moves, knights can be very tricky pieces to handle, and it is often difficult to work out where they will be able to go, two or three moves ahead.

How the pieces move

# Castling

There is one other move which concerns the pieces, and that is the *castling* move. It was added to the game, again in the fifteenth century, in order to place the king on a square where it is well protected.

It is the only move where two pieces move at once. They are the king and the king's rook (if the player is castling on the king's side of the board), or the king and the queen's rook (if the player is castling on the queen's side).

This move may only be made if the king and whichever rook is involved have not moved at all. Even if one of them has moved and then moved back to the original square, the player cannot castle. Also there must be nothing on the squares between the king and the rook. To castle, the player moves his king two squares towards the rook then places the rook on the square to which the king would have gone if it had only moved one square. Perhaps it could be said that the rook jumps in this move to the other side of the king.

Remember that a player cannot castle out of check, into check or through check. "Through check" means moving the king over a square on which it would have been in check. On the other hand, if a rook is threatened (and neither it nor the king have been moved), the player is allowed to castle to get the rook out of trouble.

Most players if they are going to castle do so early in the game. This is because the move helps to bring one of the rooks into play as well as defending the king.

Black completes her castling move on the queen's side.

**1** Black is about to castle on the queen's side. White is ready to castle on the king's side.

**2** The position after castling.

# How the pieces move
## *The Pawns*

Although they are the least valuable of the pieces, the pawns still have a very important part to play and a good chess player will always be concerned about the position of his pawns.

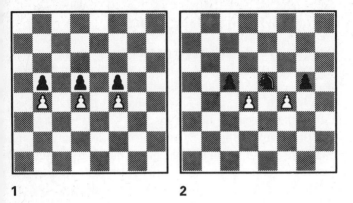

**1**          **2**

They generally move by going forward in a straight line one square at a time, but the first time they move, they have the privilege of advancing two squares if the player wishes. So when a player moves any of his pawns for the first time, he has the choice of moving them to the third rank or the fourth rank. Pawns are the only pieces which cannot go backwards.

Pawns are different from all the other pieces in that they do not capture by making their ordinary forward moves. In fact if there is an opposing pawn on a square that a pawn would otherwise be able to go to, it is not allowed to move there, or capture the piece, and we say that it is blocked. In order to capture, a pawn moves one square forward diagonally, either to its left or to its right. So unless it is at the edge of the board, each pawn has two squares on which it may possibly capture.

In diagram 1, the pawns are blocked, but in diagram 2, they may take each other. If it is white's turn to move he may capture either pawn or the knight.

# *The* En Passant *Rule*

In diagram 1, each player has moved his king's pawn. White has moved it two squares, and black has moved it one square. In diagram 2, white has moved his king's pawn to the fifth rank. This means that if black moves either his queen's pawn or his king's bishop's pawn to the third rank, white's pawn will be able to capture it. Black uses the pawn's privilege of moving his queen's pawn two squares to the fourth rank on its first move, so that it looks as if white has lost the chance to take the pawn.

To compensate for this, however, white, on *his* next move, is allowed to capture black's pawn just as though

Both players have moved twice. (The state of the game in Diagram 2)

it had only moved forward one square. But he *must* do this on his very next move, or he loses the privilege.

As diagram 3 shows, the white pawn does not go to the square to which black's pawn in fact went. It goes to the square on which the black pawn would have been had it moved one square only. This is the only capture in chess where the piece does not arrive on the square from which it has actually captured. Any pawn may be in a position to make this move.

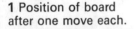

**1** Position of board after one move each.

**2** Position of board after two moves each.

**3** Position of board after three moves. Black's queen's pawn has been taken by white's king's pawn.

# *Pawn Promotion*

If a pawn reaches the other side of the board without being either blocked or captured, it becomes very important indeed, because on the eighth rank the player is able to *promote* it. That means he can exchange it for any piece of his own colour, and usually he chooses a

White 'promotes' his pawn on reaching the eighth rank.

Here the white pawns are able to queen, but the black pawns have been stopped by the white king.

queen as this is the most powerful piece. It does not matter that he still has the first queen on the board. He is allowed to have two, and even more if he can get them, but of course his opponent will do everything he can to prevent this.

Very often the last stage of the game (called the *end game*) is a struggle to see who can queen a pawn first. Once one player has an *extra* queen, he will usually be able to checkmate his opponent quite easily.

If there are two or three pawns next to each other, it will usually be easier to queen one of them than if there is just one on its own. This is because the two or three pawns can protect each other from capture. That is one reason why chess players try to avoid having "isolated pawns".

# Check and Checkmate

We have seen that a player is in check if his opponent is threatening to capture his king. If he cannot stop the check with his next move, it is checkmate and his opponent has won, since putting the other player's king in a position to be captured is the aim of the game.

There are three ways of stopping a check:
1. by moving the king;
2. by capturing the opposing piece which is giving check; and
3. by placing a piece between the king and the piece checking it.

The third way does not work where the check is given by a knight, as a knight would be able to jump over the intervening piece.

**1** Black can stop this check any of the three possible ways.

**2** There are two one-move checkmates here for white. Have you spotted them?

Answers on page 52.

The state of the game in Diagram 2, page 24.

## Reasons for Checking

The most important reason for checking is that by doing so the player hopes to force his opponent's king into checkmate, but there are other reasons too. For example, it may be that by giving check the other player has to put one of his pieces in the way to stop the check. That piece is then "pinned", and not quite so useful in the game. Sometimes, making an opponent spend a move getting out of check prevents him from making an attack in another direction.

# Discovered Check

This happens when a player moves a piece and by doing so puts his opponent's king in check from one of his other pieces. In diagram 1, if white moves his bishop, there will be a discovered check from his rook.

When you have had some practice at chess, you will be able to plan ahead, and you will sometimes be able to achieve a "double check" on your opponent's king. This happens when you move one piece to check the king, and another check from the piece behind — a discovered check — is revealed.

**1**                    **2**

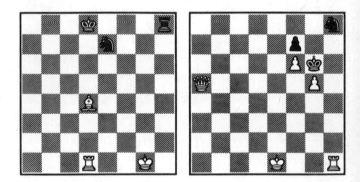

# Stalemate and Other Draws

It sometimes happens that a player is not actually in check but is unable to move without putting himself in check. Then, the position is stalemate and the game is a draw. Diagram 2 is an example of a stalemate. Black

cannot move, since of the five squares open to him, white's castle is covering three, white's queen is covering one, and a white pawn is covering the last one, so that he would be moving into check. If he captured either of the two white pawns, this would also put him in check. There is no square to which his knight can move, and his only pawn is blocked by a white pawn. Therefore – stalemate.

Stalemate is not the only way that a game of chess can be drawn. Games are sometimes drawn by "perpetual check", where one player can keep on checking his opponent every move, but cannot force him into checkmate. A game may also be a draw by repetition of moves, i.e. when the players reach the same position with the same person to move, three times.

A very common way for a game to finish is when the players simply agree to a draw, usually because neither of them thinks he can break through the other's defences.

# The Middle Game

Although a game of chess is won by checkmating the other player's king, it is usually a mistake to try to do this too early in the game, because a good opponent will have made sure that his king is very well defended – perhaps by castling. It is much better to try to capture some of the opposing pieces first, or force them to move out of the way, and *then* attack the king.

This struggle to capture pieces and break through the other player's defences is called the *middle game*, and it usually takes place in the centre of the board. The player who can control the squares in the centre of the board will be in a strong position from which to attack the king.

Black's turn to move: he could take white's knight with his bishop, for example.

# The Opening

The first few moves of a game of chess are called the *opening*, and it is in the opening that each player brings out (*develops*) his pieces, placing them on squares from which they can control the all-important centre squares.

The player who can develop his pieces more quickly than his opponent will gain more control of the centre, and therefore will have an advantage right from the beginning of the game. This is why so much thought has been given to ways of playing the first few moves. These ways are called *opening systems* or just *openings*, and many very large books have been written on the subject.

Whilst it is an advantage to learn opening systems, it is possible to play very good chess without doing so as long as these important points are kept in mind:

1  Move at least one of the pawns in front of the king and queen.
2  Place the knights and bishops on squares from which they can reach as many other squares as possible. (For example, the knight should not be at the edge of the board.)
3  Castle during the first few moves so that the king is well protected.
4  Make it possible for the rooks to come into play. Castling will also help to do this.
5  Make sure that the pieces are protecting each other but not blocking each other.
6  *Do not* bring the queen out too soon or the other player will attack it, and moves will have to be wasted to rescue it.

The state of the game
in the photograph
below.

# Special Openings

Diagram 1 shows the position after both players have played three moves of a king's side opening called the Giuoco Piano. Its title is Italian for "quiet game", and it is a *king's* side opening because it is the king's pawn that has moved. In spite of its name, this opening can lead to some very exciting chess.

In diagram 2 white has made two moves of a queen's side opening called Queen's Gambit. If black accepts the gambit he will be one pawn up, but he will have used a move to take it which he could have used to develop a piece. Also white gains more room in the centre. Of course black may decline the gambit by not taking the pawn, and do something else instead.

The Giuoco Piano and the Queen's Gambit are just two of the many opening systems that exist and each opening has many variations on the basic moves.

The situation in diagram 1.

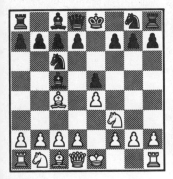

**1** Position after three moves after Giuoco Piano opening.

**1a** White has now castled to the king's side (only one of a number of possible moves).

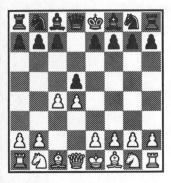

**2** Position after two moves of Queen's Gambit opening.

**2a** Black has declined the Gambit and brought out his bishop.

# Forcing Checkmate

If a player has played the opening well, and won the struggle in the middle game, he will start to think about checkmating his opponent's king.

**1** Two more moves to checkmate.

**1a** Game at checkmate.

He must try to force the king into a corner, either onto the back row or to a part of the board where it is easy to surround it. It is always more difficult to checkmate the king in the middle of the board.

In diagram 1, the white king has already been restricted to one quarter of the board, and in two more moves black should be able to checkmate it.

Sometimes there are so few pieces left on the board that it may not be possible for anyone to get checkmate. If it isn't possible, the game is a draw.

For example, can a player with a king and one piece win against a player who has only a king? The answer is yes, if the piece is a queen or a rook. If it is a pawn it will

**2** White can win – if it's his move.

**2a** White's first move to achieve checkmate – see if you can finish it!

depend on whether it is able to reach the eighth rank without being blocked by the opposing king. In diagram 2 white can win if it is his move. If it is black to move, however, the game is a draw, because the position is stalemate.

# Endgames

In an endgame, it is not always an advantage for it to be your move. In diagram 1 the player who has to move loses, because he is forced to move his king off the square where it is protecting his pawn. The other player will then be able to take the pawn and go on to promote his own.

One of the features of an endgame is that the king becomes a very active piece. The position of the king can make all the difference to the result of the game. In diagram 2 white will win, because he can take his king round the back of black's pawns and capture them one by one. Black's king is too far away to prevent it. From then on, it will be straightforward for white to queen one of his own pawns and win.

**1** If it's white to move, he will lose.

**1a** Probable finish to game in diagram 1. Note black queen now on board.

**2** White should win.

**2a** Probable finish to game in diagram 2. Note white queen now on board.

# An Interesting Endgame Position

Another interesting example of an endgame is how to win with king, knight and bishop against a king. This is possible, but very difficult indeed because the king has many ways of escape. The diagram shows the mating position which has to be reached without breaking the "fifty move rule". This rule says that if fifty moves have been played without any captures or without a pawn being moved the game is a draw. (Although sometimes in the top rank of international chess, the number of moves may be increased.)

As with the openings there are many endgame positions which chessmasters have worked out and written about. It is worth studying some of the books about them.

# Exchanges

In order to improve his position a chess player will sometimes capture one of his opponent's pieces, and in return allow his opponent to take one of his. This is

**1** Queen is offered as 'sacrifice'.

**1a** Position of pieces at checkmate.

**2** Here, white prefers to lose his knight rather than his pawn.

**2a** Position of pieces at checkmate.

known as an exchange. A good player never exchanges pieces just for the sake of doing so, but only where it leads to a better position. When thinking about an exchange you must consider very carefully just how it is going to help you.

Although pawns are the least powerful, for example, there can be situations in which the player would sacrifice what appears to be a more powerful piece such as a knight for a pawn in order to gain an advantage.

Of course, much depends on the position. In diagram 1, white is hoping to "sacrifice" his queen to black for nothing in exchange. This is unusual, since many players would only be prepared to lose their queen if they gained their opponent's queen in exchange. However, he is offering the sacrifice to get checkmate in two moves.

In diagram 2, white would rather lose his knight than his pawn, because his pawn is a very valuable one and about to become a queen.

# Pins and Forks

It is sometimes good to put an opponent at a disadvantage by pinning one of his pieces, as has already been mentioned (page 25). In diagram 1, white is pinning black's queen against his king. Black cannot evade the attack because he is not allowed to put himself in check. It is a very strong position for white. He will be able to capture the queen and only needs to lose a bishop for it.

Where one piece attacks two opposing pieces at once there is a *fork*. In diagram 2, the white queen and rook are "forked" by black's knight. White can move one piece out of danger, but black will be able to take the other one.

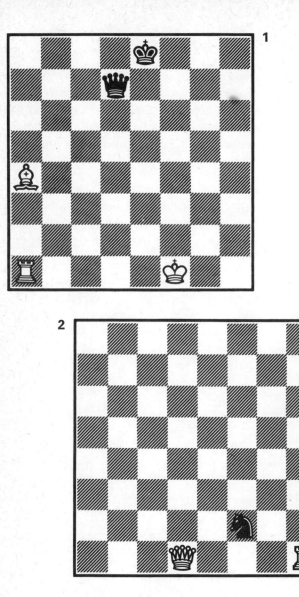

43

# *Writing Down the Game*

If you want to read chess books or to play chess by post, or to keep a record of important games, it is necessary to know how the moves are written down. There are two main ways and the one explained here is the most common one in English-speaking countries.

So that every square on the board can be given a label the board is first of all divided into two, the king's side and the queen's side, and the files are named after the pieces which are on them when the board is set up to begin the game. This is shown in diagram 1. There is the

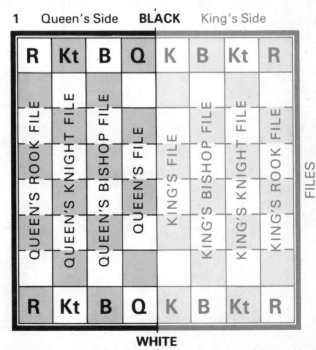

1    Queen's Side    **BLACK**    King's Side

| R | Kt | B | Q | K | B | Kt | R |

QUEEN'S ROOK FILE  QUEEN'S KNIGHT FILE  QUEEN'S BISHOP FILE  QUEEN'S FILE  KING'S FILE  KING'S BISHOP FILE  KING'S KNIGHT FILE  KING'S ROOK FILE

FILES

| R | Kt | B | Q | K | B | Kt | R |

**WHITE**

king's file and the queen's file, the king's bishop file and the queen's bishop file, and so on.

You will notice that the file which is the queen's bishop file for white is still the queen's bishop file when the board is viewed from black's side. The files have the same names for each player.

This is not true of the ranks, because each player calls the rank nearest to him one and the rank furthest away eight. Therefore the square which would be queen's rook one if white's move were being written down would be queen's rook eight if it were black's move. This can be seen in diagram 2.

**2**          **BLACK**

| QR1 QR8 | QKt1 QKt8 | QB1 QB8 | Q1 Q8 | K1 K8 | KB1 KB8 | KKt1 KKt8 | KR1 KR8 |
|---------|-----------|---------|-------|-------|---------|-----------|---------|
| QR2 QR7 | QKt2 QKt7 | QB2 QB7 | Q2 Q7 | K2 K7 | KB2 KB7 | KKt2 KKt7 | KR2 KR7 |
| QR3 QR6 | QKt3 QKt6 | QB3 QB6 | Q3 Q6 | K3 K6 | KB3 KB6 | KKt3 KKt6 | KR3 KR6 |
| QR4 QR5 | QKt4 QKt5 | QB4 QB5 | Q4 Q5 | K4 K4 | KB4 KB5 | KKt4 KKt5 | KR4 KR5 |
| QR5 QR4 | QKt5 QKt4 | QB5 QB4 | Q5 Q4 | K5 K4 | KB5 KB4 | KKt5 KKt4 | KR5 KR4 |
| QR6 QR3 | QKt6 QKt3 | QB6 QB3 | Q6 Q3 | K6 K3 | KB6 KB3 | KKt6 KKt3 | KR6 KR3 |
| QR7 QR2 | QKt7 QKt2 | QB7 QB2 | Q7 Q2 | K7 K2 | KB7 KB2 | KKt7 KKt2 | KR7 KR2 |
| QR8 QR1 | QKt8 QKt1 | QB8 QB1 | Q8 Q1 | K8 K1 | KB8 KB1 | KKt8 KKt1 | KR8 KR1 |

**WHITE (red)**

45

# A Written Game

Now that every square on the board can be named all that is usually necessary to record a move is to say which piece is moving and the square to which it is moving. To do this the initial letters of the pieces are used, but knight is written Kt so that it cannot be confused with king. (It is also sometimes written N – for (K)night, ignoring the 'K'.)

In diagram 1 each player has moved his king's pawn to the fourth rank and developed one of his knights. The game would be written down:

|   | *White* | *Black* |
|---|---------|---------|
| 1 | P – K4 | P – K4 |
| 2 | Kt – KB3 | Kt – QB3 |

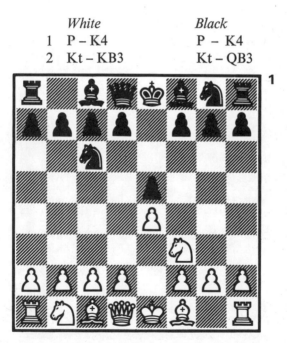

**1**

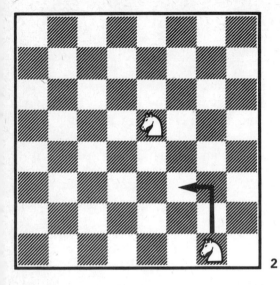

**2**

However, Kt – KB3 would not be enough to record the move shown in diagram 2 since both knights can reach KB3. To make it clear which is meant, the move would be written Kt$_{(Kt1)}$ – KB3 or even KKt – KB3.

Ch written after a move means check while e.p. means en passant. Where there is a capture the word "takes" is represented by an x. Pawn takes pawn en passant would be written P x P e.p. Castles king's side is written O – O and castles queen's side O – O – O.

# A Game Played by Napoleon

Here is a famous game for you to try. It is very short, and was played between the Emperor Napoleon and Claire, Comtesse de Rémusat, in 1804. The Comtesse was lady-in-waiting to the Empress Josephine, and her letters and memoirs tell of life at the French court at that time, as well as many anecdotes about Napoleon himself.

| | Napoleon (White) | Comtesse de Rémusat (Black) |
|---|---|---|
| 1 | Kt – QB3 | P – K4 |
| 2 | Kt – KB3 | P – Q3 |
| 3 | P – K4 | P – KB4 |
| 4 | P – KR3 | P × P |
| 5 | QKt × P | Kt – QB3 |
| 6 | Kt$_{(B3)}$ – Kt5 | P – Q4 |
| 7 | Q – R5 Ch | P – KKt3 |
| 8 | Q – B3 | Kt – R3 |
| 9 | Kt – B6 Ch | K – K2 |
| 10 | Kt × QP Ch | K – Q3 |
| 11 | Kt – K4 Ch | K × Kt |
| 12 | B – B4 Ch | K × B |
| 13 | Q – Kt3 Ch | K – Q5 |
| 14 | Q – Q3 Checkmate | |

# Clocks and Computers

Experienced chess players take a long time over their games because before they make each move they see and consider many possibilities. They always think several moves ahead, working out what they might do, and what their opponent might do.

For this reason there will usually be a time limit on a chess match. For example, each player may have to play forty moves in two hours. This makes sure that by the time four hours have passed the game should be finished, or at least drawing to a conclusion.

So that each player's time can be recorded separately, chess clocks have been invented. They are really two clocks in one, and when a player has completed his move he presses the mechanism which stops his clock and sets his opponent's going. If a player does not play all his moves in the time allowed, he loses the game.

A chess clock, used to time moves in a tournament.

Nowadays many computers can play chess. They can be programmed not to repeat their mistakes so that, just like people, they improve with practice.

Chess Challenger 7 – A computerised chess board – it will play against either beginners or experienced players.

A video chess game

**Index**

---

*Page 24 – answers*

The knight takes the bishop; checkmate; or, the queen
goes to QKt3.